VICTORIAN
STORIES 'ROUND A
DARTMOOR HEARTH

TODD GRAY

THE
MINT
PRESS

First published in Great Britain by The Mint Press, 2001

ISBN 1-903356-20-2

Cataloguing in Publication Data
CIP record for this title is available from the British Library

The Mint Press
18 The Mint
Exeter, Devon
England EX4 3BL

Text and cover design by Delphine Jones

Printed and bound in Great Britain
by Short Run Press Ltd, Exeter.

CONTENTS

INTRODUCTION

'Christmas Readings: Round the Kitchen Fire' was written by 'Tickler' and published in *The Devon Weekly Times* in its Christmas issue of 21 December 1866. The author has not been identified but was a regular contributor to the newspaper. He could well have been on the staff. It is accompanied by 'Pixie-led: A Christmas Adventure on Haldon' which was published in *The Devon Weekly Times* on 24 December 1895. The author was anonymous.

Through most of the year local newspapers reprinted stories which had already appeared in national publications but readers were given local stories at Christmas. Generally the national stories were fairly long and mostly serialised over several weeks. In contrast, the local stories were shorter and appeared in one special issue, generally the last before Christmas.

The main part of this collection was printed as a long narrative in an entire Christmas piece in 1866. It is supplemented by another story published nearly thirty years later. 'Tickler', the first writer, also included a number of 'conundrums' including:

When is Exeter Guildhall like a stable?
When the Mayor's (mare) in it.

Why is Father Peter at the corner of North Street like a careful housewife?
Because he takes care of the keys.

Why is going to Exeter Theatre like the year 1865?
Because it is past time (pastime).

The Devon Weekly Times was aimed, to a certain degree, at an Exeter audience and the stories of Dartmoor reflect an urban interest in the moor; that the city's inhabitants had only a slight familiarity is borne out by the stories. A particular Victorian favourite was the legend of the pixies on the moor and this was brought out by several of the writers. The stories were meant to reflect the good-natured quality of the festive season and encourage a sense of duty and charity to those members of society who were less fortunate.

CHRISTMAS READINGS
'ROUND THE KITCHEN FIRE

TICKLER

1866

And why not 'Round the kitchen fire?' You are not so weak, gentle reader, as to be prepossessed in favour of the gentilities of life, are you? Not you. They are so often such counterfeits of nature that I am sure you and I are glad to get away from them – just as the genuine heart and simple mind prefers the blue sky, the green fields, and the bright flowers, to the imitations thereof, to be seen in a theatre.

Why not 'Round the kitchen fire' when the blazing faggot crackles joyously, the bright flame leaps merrily upwards, and faces all about it are beaming with hospitality and kindness? Better 'Round the kitchen fire', however humble, with these genuine elements for our Christmas companions, than round the drawing-room fire, with all the fashion, display, luxury and hollowness that the daintiest dandy in the universe may desire.

Again, why not 'Round the kitchen fire'? For did not the old Romans consecrate their hearths to Penates – the divinest of their gods; and, as though to protest on behalf of all posterity against conventional shams being introduced into the sacredest of places – that of Home – they had one common room for the enjoyment of all their dearest domestic pleasures and joys.

Oh! I love the kitchen – not, I am bound to say, the kitchen soiled by the cook and made uncomfortably suspicious by the nocturnal visits of 'Sarah's young man' but the kitchen, say of the old farm house, where the fire burns on the hearth, in which there is space to turn round, where there is verge and scope enough for a country dance, and where you get good hunting ground for a run after the girls preparatory to the inevitable kiss under the mistletoe. With views so simple as these (and, it may be, from an elevated fashionable point of view, so very heterodox), is it any wonder that I accepted, with alacrity, an invitation to spend the Christmas with a Moorland farmer and his merry family?

No matter when and where. This much I have no objection to tell the reader – it was at a period when snow lay deep upon the ground, when ice for healthy skating purposes was inches thick on pond, lake, and river, and when there was a proper break between the seasons, ere Nature had become so capricious as to send us strawberries, raspberries, violets and other summer fruits and spring flowers, in time honoured 'bleak December'.

As to where I enjoyed my holiday, it will be sufficient for me to say that it was at a place not quite a hundred miles from 'Widdicombe-in-the-Moor'. 'How did I get there?' Well, that is another question that I do not feel called upon for any very definite reply. I did, however, get there – through snow and wind – after many toilsome ascents and hazardous descents – and when I heard the welcome bark of the old house dog, and the cheery voice of my Moorland friend, as he tugged at my snow-covered coat, and enquired over and over again

'Well, how be ee? How de'e zeem to be?'

I inwardly thanked Providence that I had arrived safely at my journey's end, and that I should not have the honour to be immortalized in a newspaper article, with the significant and melancholy heading of 'Lost in the Snow'.

My host's house was of granite; and so also, it seemed to me, was his constitution, but most certainly not his heart. His manners were not polished, in the world's sense, but they were genuine manners – the outward and visible signs of an inward and natural grace, goodness and tenderness.

He was well matched in his spouse, and his three 'darters' and one son were genuine 'chips of the old blocks' – true as steel, as natural as the snow-topped tors and hills about them, and as free as the winds that play over their grand old summits. They were too far away to come often to the city, and it was good for them it was so, for I have often observed that, when our 'country cousins' lose their natural and healthy tastes, and take to the gentilities, they make a sad bungle of it.

It was early on Christmas Eve that I arrived at — Barton. I pass over the shaking of hands all round – the pain in the wrists which I suffered for days afterwards as the result thereof. And the comfortable tea, such as before nor since I certainly never enjoyed with so keen a relish. After tea, and at a given time, the labourers and the servants arrived. As they came into the kitchen they made respectful bows and curtseys to 'master' and 'missus', to 'young master', 'the young missuses' and to 'Mr Tickler'.

Need I say that the spacious kitchen was decorated with holly and mistletoe, and that the broad-backed hams, suspended here and there from the well-smoked rafters, did not in any way detract from the festive appearance of the place.

'Bring in the faggots, Bob,' said the host in a voice that indicated a determination to be completely jolly, and not to give a thought to such mundane considerations as the prices of wool, mutton or 'wots'. And the 'faggots' were brought in, and piled up, and up, until I thought they would almost reach the chimney top. It was a veritable bonfire.

'Dra vore, Mr Tickler,' said friend Giles, the oldest of the labourers present.

'No thank you Giles, I'll dra back, I think,' said I.

'Tha yet too much for ee, zir?' enquired the considerate Giles.

'Well, I rather think it is,' I replied. The

first hour was appropriately dedicated to 'zyder hot' – an agreeable and exhilarating beverage - and to gossip.

I found Giles, who sat nearest to me, an intelligent and communicative companion.

'Naw, Tom French? I shude rather think I did, zir,' said he in reply to my question.

'And a brave feller he was,' he continued. 'Tis quite true he did naw every bog and tor from Beliver to Dewerstone, almost every holt and hover that could harbour a fox or an otter between Heytor Rock and Tolchmoor Gate.'

It was also quite true, Giles said, that, after Mr Bulteel had turned adrift a lot of

French and English foxes on the moor, and the farmer's roosts were incessantly assailed, and despoiled. So much was this so that Farmer – who had been plundered by the varmint in a very wholesale manner, indeed, wrote to Lord John Russell, who was then in office, but who had, of course, no power or jurisdiction over Dartmoor foxes, to this effect:

'Sir John Russell,

I shude thank you if you plaize to com to bentwitching and Hunt these darned foxes, for I have lost two lambs again.'

'Did his Lordship come and hunt the foxes?' I enquired of Giles.

'Not ee, zur,' was his reply, and he added that the farmer was not able to preserve his geese or his lambs until he hired Tom French to kill the 'darned voxes'.

'Come, Mr Tickler, you've had gossip enough I think with Giles,' said one of the young ladies, in sweet tones of gentle rebuke. I humbly bowed my head in submission.

'I think you are quite right, my dear, 'said my host to his fair and rosy daughter, and he continued, 'There is nothing like harmony to start with, so I'll call upon Giles for a song'.

Accordingly Giles, having taken a 'long pull and a strong pull' at the foaming 'mug' that was considerately passed to him, and wiped his mouth scientifically with his sleeve, sang in a powerful but somewhat husky voice a ditty the words of which I cannot pretend to give, but every sense of which ended:

> *With holly and ivy*
> *Be green and so gay,*
> *We deck up our houses*
> *As fresh as the day.*

A country dance followed for there was a rustic fiddler, of the most energetic character, present – which everybody enjoyed and then 'round the kitchen fire' we again assembled, our sides aching with laughter, and our festive hearts thumping violently but delightfully with the excitement of the dance.

After supper, we again sat round the hearth, and more wood was piled up.

'Soce, pass round the mug.' So said our worthy host.

'Mug' was accordingly passed round, and duly honoured, after which I ventured to say that I thought a story or two would entertain the company.

My observation was greeted with loud 'hear, hears', and stamping of feet; and when, in continuation of my little speech (for I had so far forgotten myself as to 'get upon my legs' and address 'My friends all' in a somewhat oratorical fashion) – I suggested that Farmer – should begin, the kitchen rang with applause, and the blazing faggots sent up festive fireworks of a very luminous and sparkling character indeed.

'Maggy, my dear, get me my pipe, for I can never tell a story without en.' Said the 'founder of the feast' to his youngest daughter, who obeyed his request with an alacrity of filial affection that was good to see.

Having lit his pipe, and puffed upwards to the rafters sundry little gyrating clouds of smoke, our host thus related:

THE FAIRY
AND
THE FARMER

TICKLER

1866

You don't believe in fairies or pixies, I believe, Mr Tickler? Well, I do. I've seen 'em often on the moor, of summer nights, dancing right merrily, and singing soft and sweet like an Eolian harp.

In the morning, afore the dew was taken up by the sun, I've seen the 'fairy rings' where they've 'trod the light fantastic' the night before, and I've had my nose a-pinched, often and often, by the mischievous and funny little devils, when I've taken a nap on the heather in the forenoon after dinner.

I was summoned to Exeter as a juryman at the Winter Assizes in 18-. It was a very long Assize, and there had been many very heavy and dreadful cases. The business lasted right up to Christmas Eve. About five o'clock I observed that the Lord Jidge got a little fidgety – for he was evidently wanting to be off with the 'little lord Jidges'. Even Jidges, I suppose, have got 'little ones' who like to see father home to keep Christmas.

Well, all at once his Lordship said

'Brother Bobkins, I shall take no more cases – tis Christmas Eve – and what cases are left must be made remnants (remanets) of'.

All the long-wigged gentlemen seemed quite glad, and it was as much as I could do to prevent my fellow jurymen from bursting forth into a cheer, for they all wanted to be off to keep Christmas.

I left the Court, however, with a somewhat heavy heart, for I knew I couldn't get to my place that night, which, of all others in the 'old house at home' we always keep up with much joy and gladsomeness. Well, after tea at my inn (where I will say I was made uncommonly comfortable) I took a walk down High Street, and looked into the butchers' shops.

Never did I see such beautiful meat before. I looked at it again and again, and at the pale faces that were near me, on many of which I read words like these:

'I wish I could see a joint of that beautiful beast on my table tomorrow!'

Ah! Mr Tickler, and I wished it too most devoutly. After feasting my eyes for a good while – my thoughts still running upon home – I walked here and there; and, among other things, which I dearly like to see, I went and had a look at the Cathedral by moonlight.

Twas a beautiful sight, and strange to say, when I was gazing intently at it all at once I saw tripping across the green, near the splendid old building, the pixy, or 'Fairy Queen' that I had often seen on the moor of moonlight nights when looking after my sheep.

I couldn't help an expression of surprise and delight, but she - well, I think she is a she, although I am not quite certain as to the sex – put her little finger upon her little mouth, and beckoned me to follow. I did so. She led me through a narrow lane, then across a street, then into another narrow lane, and then down – oh! such a miserable, dirty street with the gas lights looking in the fog like so many Jack o' the lanterns. Before a house, or rather a tumble down building, 'Fairy Queen' stopped; and, pointing earnestly to a little child at the doorway, bade me, by a gentle gesticulation which I could not fail to understand, speak with her.

I entered into conversation with the child, and found her remarkably intelligent. Whilst speaking to her a benevolent 'sick visitor', whom I knew to be a good fellow, came up and said:

'Farmer, come with me, for I should like you to see the prospects that some people in this rich city have of a 'merry Christmas'.' Accordingly in I went; and I shall not forget in a hurry the scene that I there looked upon. Sitting by a grate – I will not say fire, for in the presence of this blazing ashen faggot it would be a libel to call it a fire – sitting, then, by a handful of fire, was a pale-faced woman of, as I should judge, between 30 and 40 years of age.

She had evidently once been a pretty woman, and there was a light in her eyes that showed that love and hope still dwelt in her heart. She was sewing away as fast as her thin fingers could sew, and every now and then she would look up, with a sad but loving smile to a girl, who was sitting by her side, and who likewise was engaged in making some article of dress. The maiden appeared to me about eighteen years old – very pretty, and very much like her mother – as I afterwards discovered.

In a bed, fast asleep, in the same room, were two little boys, locked in each other's arms, and apparently dreaming of 'Happy Christmas'. All this I saw at a glance; also that the room was almost bare of furniture, but yet that it was scrupulously clean. I apologised for my intrusion, but said that I had been led there by our 'Fairy Queen'. Mother and daughter did not appear to understand this; and the former, looking kindly into my face, said:

'Sir, you are very welcome, although I have not the pleasure of knowing you.'

I was asked to sit down, which I did; and the 'sick visitor' having told 'em who I was, where I came from, and what I had come to Exeter for, we all got into a confidential chat.

I soon learnt that the poor woman had married early one 'whom she loved –oh! so dearly' – and that just after the fourth child was born the husband died, leaving wife and family unprovided for. They had 'seen better days' – there was no mistake about that, for the language and manner of both were sufficient evidence thereof. As gently as I could I drew from them that the Christmas dinner depended on what the work of that day would produce, and that was a sum I'm ashamed to mention. I ventured, after a good many awkward hems and haws, to say 'I was very well off', that I had a good many sheep and pigs; that the harvests lately had been capital; and, if they would let me pay for a good dinner, I should be so pleased for, said I (with a smile, and the two women laughed outright) I'd bet a guinea the youngsters so sweetly sleeping in the bed were dreaming of figgy pudden!

Both mother and daughter thanked me very much, and I slipped something – well, no matter what – into the hand of the young girl. The sum was sufficient to buy a good Christmas dinner, and that's enough on that head.

Well, I had scarcely done this when I heard soft footsteps and whispering outside the door. I observed the eyes of mother and daughter suddenly to light up with wonderful brilliancy.

'I know he's come. I'm sure he is. I told you so. I dreamt he would!'

Such were the rapid exclamations of the mother to the daughter.

'Dear mother!'

'Dear son!' were the next words I

heard, and then, before I could say 'Jack Robinson' I noticed a fine stalwart young fellow in sailor's garb, hugging then mother and then daughter, as though he would crumple them to pieces.

Then there was kissing and sobbing, and great joy. I must say I could not help crying like a child myself; and now, for the first time, I observed another fine young sailor standing near me.

'Why Bob, is that you?' exclaimed the mother.

'Yes, tis me, my dears,' said the young fellow addressed, and then there was a hearty shaking of hands all round.

For the young girl there was something more – a long kiss of ardent affection, followed by a deep blush and silence. But to make a long story short, soce, let me tell you that the first fine young man was the poor widow's son, and that he had left home to seek his fortune on the stormy sea, just after his father's death. The other was his companion, and Lucy's (for that was the name of the pretty young girl) betrothed.

Both had gone away on a Christmas Eve, and had sailed in the same ship. Often had the brave young fellows been given up for lost; but, after surviving one wreck, and escaping by a hair's breadth another, they had come home, after many years of ocean life, to make their loving friends happy on Christmas Eve.

As I rose to bid mother and daughter, and the newcomers 'Goodbye, and all of 'ee a happy Christmas' they said in the heartiest manner and with such joy in their united voices as I shall never forget 'Yes sir, we shall indeed have a happy Christmas!'

At that moment I noticed 'Fairy Queen' at the door. Dignity and triumph sat on her little brow, as she beckoned me with her wand to follow her. I obeyed. She led me out into the main street; and, as she kissed her hand, in token of farewell (for fairies never speak to mortals), she seemed to me to say

'Farmer, you have seen that which, amidst all the glory and beauty of your native hills and dales, you had never seen before; that which shows you that, in this Christian country, and in rich cities, there is much long-suffering and loving-kindness among the poor – suffering much too often overlooked by those who ought not to overlook it, by those who feel more for the people abroad that they do for their poor neighbours at home.'

•

'Mr Tickler, since the night that I was pixy-led in Exeter, I have never given the passen anything for the Fatagonians (for whom he annually preaches) but I give what I can spare to my own poor countrymen; and this I have resolved never to part with – namely, my belief in human love and goodness, nor in the dear little fairies of my native hills.'

Just as our host had finished his story I observed that Gile's chin had dropped on his ample bosom, and that he appeared to be in a doze.

'Giles has had his quantum,' said our hostess, who seemed to be familiar with the old gentleman's habits.

'See him home, Bob!' said our host to his son.

Accordingly Bob took the old man gently by the arm, and I offered to become the other prop.

'Good night measter (said Giles) and all the good and kind company, and my ee have a Merry Christmas and a Happy New Year!'

'Thank ee, Giles, and I wish you and yours a Merry Christmas and a Happy New Year!' said one and all in return for the old man's kind wishes. The cold air somewhat restored Giles, but he was uncommonly shaky on his 'pins' as Robert observed. The old man confidentially told us 'that his wive and darter were Methodys and that there would be a jolly row when he got hoam.'

We reached the cottage at last, and to my discomfort Gile's prediction was abundantly verified. Both mother and daughter asked him 'What portion drunkards had in the next world?' which he answered by saying he hoped as good as 'Farmer –'s nice warm kitchen, supper and zider-hot.'

This was too much for the young girl, who, on hearing the profane remark, burst into tears. Upon seeing his daughter crying, Giles rose from his seat, and, advancing with an uncommonly unsteady gait to the weeping damsel, said:

'Betsy, my dear, doant ee cry; tidden as ef I'd a com hoam in likker, you naw!'

(Bob whispered to me - 'Hark at the old man. Why he's a drunk as a drane.')

We wished Giles good night, and begged mother and daughter to see the old man to bed, which they said they would do after they had prayed 'that the brand may be plucked from the burning!'

We soon returned to the barton, and rejoined the happy family 'round the kitchen fire.'

One of the young ladies – Miss Judith – was called upon for a song or a story. She said 'I have here in manuscript a story by Lady Bowring, who is very fond of the moor, and her ladyship, having once rested in our parlour in one of her rambles, told it to me, and at my request very kindly wrote it out and sent it to me.

'Shall I read it?'

'Certainly' we all said in one breath.

Miss Judith read as follows

PIXIE LED

LADY BOWRING

It was on a summer's evening, when we somewhat wearily pursued our way towards one of those quaint old country mansions which are occasionally found in some of the least frequented though beautiful spots which may be discovered among our moorland scenery.

The day had been oppressively warm, and as by far the least tiresome portion of the road had been traversed

soon after leaving Exeter, we were more
disposed to complain of the narrow,
stony and frequently precipitous lanes
which lead to the higher regions of the
county. Our usually willing steed
appeared to suffer even more than
ourselves from the toils of the journey.

So weary, indeed, was our little
grey, that we were induced to allow
him for awhile to proceed at his own
pace, and as the cool evening breeze
from Dartmoor stirred the bending
grasses, tall fox gloves and waving
brackens which lined the hedgerows,
the beauty of the evening stole over us,
and so deeply were we plunged into
the reveries which the hour and the

scene inspired that we were somewhat startled when a small child, springing from some unseen nook, suddenly addressed us with an enquiry not unusual in the rural districts as to the time of day.

Having informed him the hour, we were led more closely to scan features which seemed to belong to one much older than his size betokened. A small, pale, wizened face, with a sharp expression was before us, the mouth was at the same time marked by malice and humour, and the character was borne out by that of the twinkling dark eyes, in which we soon observed that there lurked a fund of merriment.

'How far is it to Merlin Park? Do you know the way?' we asked of our new acquaintance.

'I lives home by', replied the young urchin 'and you ban't many a mile vrom 'em'.

At this moment a turn of the road opened on the left; the hoary stones, the ferny brakes, and hanging woods of the romantic spot we sought. We heard the music of the river as an accompaniment to the sigh of the evening breeze; and desirous no longer to delay our arrival, we enlisted the services of the lad and accompanied by him soon reached our destination.

Having handed our tired horse to a

female servant, she provided a warm mash and every attention prudence and kindness could suggest. Although conscious that we ourselves also required repose and refreshment, and aware that we were the expected guests of the lady then occupying the mansion, a peculiar fascination prevented us from enjoying the welcome that awaited us, and having avoided a meeting with our fair hostess, we cheerfully availed ourselves of the guidance of the pale-faced child, who promised to conduct us to 'Pixie rings' and 'Pixie wells' and above all, to the gloomy spot where the devil, having embraced the witch, left her to stand forever a withered monument, bearing on her bosom traces of the smouldered ashes of a fire enkindled by the contact of those burning lips.

The young imp fulfilled his promises, and now in the gloaming we were carefully threading our way over the steep mossy ground. It is encumbered by huge weather-stained and lichen-adorned boulders, around and into the crevices of which the roots of the many gigantic trees have worked their tortuous way, as though they found in the granite masses a holdfast against the winter's winds and storms.

We had reached the grassy level of the Park, and were in view of the dwelling house, when, through the increasing gloom, we observed a lady approaching us, and supposing it to be our hostess, were preparing apologies for our non-appearance at the house, when she accosted us.

She wore a white straw hat, adorned with violets and streamers of the same colour, and from beneath it flowed in luxuriant tresses an abundance of wavy golden hair. Even the uncertain light could not entirely veil the sparkle of her hazel eyes, nor the brilliant carmine of her rounded cheek. Her dress, devoid of crinoline, was simple in style, and its hue seemed to harmonise with the shadowy neutral tint which now overspread the landscape.

So completely had the appearance,

voice, manner and address of our amiable hostess been simulated, that we readily fell into the delusion that she had joined us, and, although both fatigued and leery, as she made no allusion to our arrival some hours previously, we scrupulously avoided the subject, fearing we might have caused some inconvenience by the delay.

But as we moved on over hill and dale, and wound past brook and mead, and by church tower and desolate hamlet, sheltering beneath the giant hills, we observed that light was called up by the presence of our visitor, to illumine our path and the various objects presented to view.

And still we proceeded further and further, until at length by narrow path, through yellow gorse, and purple heather, with difficulty tracing our weary way through rocks and craggy masses of granite, we reached the summit of a lofty mountain, from which a glorious view burst upon our sight.

In the distance were seen tors and massive rocks, half obscured in grey mist; but sunshine fell upon the nearer slopes, the neighbouring town, and the lonely farmsteads, which lay bathed in morning radiance and a rainbow arch of brilliant colours spanned a somewhat stormy sky. Silently, but admiringly, we gazed upon this picture of varied beauty. Our wanderings were over, and for some moments we seemed to live a charmed life in the presence of such sublimity; but with a sense of rest there came also that of chilliness.

Did we dream or were we waking? We rubbed our eyes, and stretched our benumbed limbs to find that, sheltered by an overhanging rock, we had indeed passed the night upon one of the Dartmoor hills. Dazed and shivering we rose from our stony bed – the lady was not to be seen – the whisht boy had vanished.

The sun had risen, and his sparkling beams now irradiated the dew drops which glistened around like thousands of diamonds. We were glad to restore circulation to our chilled frames by making our way as best we might to Merlin Park; and as we retraced our steps over the blooming uplands, musical with the hum of bees and listened to the herdsman's shout in the valley beneath, we mused on the strange circumstances of our nocturnal adventure.

As we drew near to the habitations of men, opportunities occurred of enquiring of our strange companions of the night. The beautiful female was not be found; and, as our friend at the park, although somewhat alarmed at our absence, had not quitted the house after nightfall, we fancy that she existed only in our imaginations.

As to the boy – a very Puck – he had been seen by the shepherds, at break of bay, endeavouring to misdirect the flocks. The hedgers had tried to catch him, that they might punish him for hiding their tools, but he mockingly eluded their efforts, and bounding skilfully over every obstacle, was soon out of sight. In the village many were the tales that were whispered of his elfish pranks; but, bent on overturning the newly-filled kettles and buckets at the fountain, the woman had assembled in such numbers that they had chased him away.

Although heard of in all directions, the urchin could never be secured or tracked to a settlement, and when at length, after our prolonged wanderings, we found ourselves comfortably established at the old Moorland house, and came to talk over with our kind friend the perils of the night, unable to account for our aberrations in any other way, we thought it safest to acknowledge that we must have been Pixie led, and that our guide had been no other than the Pixie King.

•

'Come Polly dear, (said our kind hostess to the daughter sitting near her) you can sing nicely. Do ee give us a song – that's a dear.'

'Well, mother,' said Miss Polly – Polly was really a charming girl - 'I have just learnt a new ditty, written by a very clever Exeter gentleman, whose poems and powers of improvisation many have heard with delight, and I will, if you please, do my best, to sing it.'

'Bravo,' cried Polly's father, and 'Bravo' echoed all Polly's friends.

A CHRISTMAS CAROL

J.P.

The merry old time's come again,

All hail! Father Christmas, your hand;

May thine be a jovial reign,

May plenty abound in the land;

May the peasant as well as the peer,

The employed as well as those who employ,

With store of good holiday cheer,

Thy bountiful season enjoy.

Then hurrah! for the merry old time.

May the blessing of peace still remain

In our happy and glorious isle;

May rebellion's stern head ne'er again
Be uplifted thro' Fenain guile;
May the rich to the poor freely give,
Of their wealth only stewards are they,
And remember that 'Live and let live'
Is a maxim we all should obey.
So hurrah! for the jolly old time.

May our senators ponder with care,
'Ere they send forth the 'Law of the land';
And (provided tis honest and fair)
Each Briton will join hand in hand
In support both of Church and of State,
Our Queen and our great constitution;
Irish traitors will find it's too late
For a 'Physical force' revolution.
Then hurrah! for the merry old time.

Have we grievances? Want we redress?
Not with pikes or with swords shall be gain it;
Perseverance and hope – nothing less,
And depend on it boys we'll obtain it;
By the strong force of reason – not arms,
But means suicidal at best;
For a country devoured by alarms,
In its commerce must needs be oppressed,
So hurrah! for the jolly old time.

There is much that remains to be done;
What of that? We have hearts stout and
*   true;*
We may have an eclipse of the sun,
Twill yet glorious burst on our view.
E'en tho' clouds for a while may obscure
The bright prospect, and render it dim;

For a time we must wait and endure,

So avaunt! Shadows dreary and grim,

And hurrah! for the merry old time.

The bigot fanatic may scowl!

On the pleasures of life as they pass;

He may deem himself wise as an owl,

But I hold him an ignorant ass.

Trust in Providence – keep a look out,

Do our duty – what can we do more?

And I trust, without shadow of doubt,

We may all keep the 'Wolf from the door'.

So hurrah! for the merry old time.

Good people, I now wish ye all

Merry Christmas and Happy New Year!

High and low, rich and poor, great and small,

God speed ye, and give ye good cheer.

Oh! may joy in your dwellings abound.

And contentment adorn each fireside;

And with blessings thus scattered around,

Feel for those who've such blessings denied.

So hurrah! for the merry old time.

'Why, Bob,' said his father, 'I'm blessed if we haven't forgotten you, my boy.'

Bob smiled, and scratched his head.

'Come, come,' said our host - 'Tis your turn, you know, so give us something – either a stave or a story.'

Bob rose from his seat and said: 'Ladies and gentlemen, when Sir John Bowring accompanied her ladyship here, as my sister Polly has just observed, he took a walk with me to see the view of yonder tor; and, on his way, amongst other things, the honourable knight told me a story, which I think I can relate almost word for word.'

The story was thus told

THE SECRET

SIR JOHN BOWRING

'I kanw'd twas he – for I zeed'n in the browse!'

'Zeed what?'

'Nort that I'll thee on. I can kip my awn secret.'

'Naw, Jim, that ban't kind. You mus'n have no secrets from me.'

And James, having awakened Betty's curiosity, did not satisfy it, but shook his head, and left the kitchen without saying another word.

Betty threw herself down on the settle by the fire. She was very angry, and even more vexed than angry.

'Well! I cudn't hav blieved it ov Jim.'

She leaned back against the wall, wept bitterly, and, having wiped away with her apron the flood of tears that had run down her cheeks, she covered her face, and said again and again, 'O, Jim! Jim! You cannot luv me, Jim!'

But Jim did love her notwithstanding. He had a rough way with him, but his heart was sound. Betty did not really mistrust him, but why did he not trust her? What could be the secret, what could the mystery be?

What was there that he ought to conceal? To conceal from her to whom he had often said that his great delight was to tell her everything: that there was only one in the world to whom he could tell everything – and that she was that one?

Then all sorts of fancies perplexed her. Who, what could he have seen? It must have been a visitor of evil omen. He had heard, he must have heard, something two awful to tell.

Very strange thoughts float through the mind of a betrothed girl; but the thought that got the uppermost was that the banns which had been ordered for the coming Sunday were to be forbidden. How what Jim had 'zeed in the browse' was, or could be, connected with the forbidding of the banns was by no means clear; but it not being clear did not make it a whit the less alarming.

In fact, our misty thoughts are those which perplex and plague us most. We easily lose ourselves in the twilight of doubt, or the darkness of uncertainty. Berry was very, very unhappy. She wept anew, she wrung her hands, again she threw her apron over her face, and said 'O, Jim! Jim! I cud'n hav blieved it of yu, Jim!'

Her mother came in, saw her daughter sitting in the settle, seeming ill at ease, her apron upon her face.

'Why, Bett! What's the matter? What's a cum tu'ee? I've a bin to the passen, an 'a paid the clerk. You don't look vitty. Why be so wisht? Tis all reart.'

Betty let drop the apron, which she held in her hand, seized her mother's, and said:

'Aw! Muther, muther!'

What, indeed, could the matter be? The old woman thought that consolation, if not explanation, was to be found somewhere, and most probably in Jim. So she went out to hunt for Jim, found him, told him something was amiss with Bett.

He must come, 'Nobody but he would du.'

So they came to the house together, but the mother soon left the young people to themselves.

James sat himself down on the settle. He took Betty by the hand.

'What is it? What is it, Bet?'

'O, Jim! Jim! Who did yu zee in the browse?'

'THE WHITE WITCH.'

But the banns were put in. Nobody forbad the banns. The young couple were married. Go to Vuzzy Down, and you may see their children gathering wortle berries.

•

I had forgotten to say that one of the company was a 'fellow of infinite jest' from the old city. He had been winking fun throughout his wicked-looking eyes all the night. I ventured, therefore, to call on my friend, whom I will name 'Tom Funnygrig' for a tale.

Accordingly he gave the following:

BEFORE THE BOARD

TOM FUNNYGRIG

It was very wrong of me, but I really couldn't help it.

I suppose it was on account of my having read the eccentricities – to say the least of them – of Mr Bumble that I did it, but I did do it.

'Did what? Why I became a pauper, and applied for relief.'

'You don't say so!'

'Yes, I do say so. I became a pauper, and went in for pauper's pay.'

'Where?'

'No, no, I shan't tell ee where, but I'll say it was in a city not a hundred miles from Exeter. How did I come to do it? Well, I'll answer that outright - 'twas for a spree. It happened on the day before Christmas and I agreed with Jack Larkins, Joe Jolly and Ned Rattler, that I'd dress up in a suit of dilapidated fustian, and go in before their 'vosships' for relief. I shall never forget the fun.

Twas awfully cold standing in the outer room for two mortal hours, as I was compelled to do, but I did it like a trump. The old women – and there were a lot of 'em present – enjoyed a monopoly of the fire, and the old men nudged and pushed up against each other, as though friction would keep 'em warm.

Well, my turn came at last. My name was called, and in I went. Their 'vosships' were men of all ages, trades, professions and aspects.

'Your name young man?'

'Bob Ridley', was my reply.

'Old Bob Ridley', enquired a red-faced, pleasant-looking man, who laughed consumedly at the joke.

'Not old,' I said, 'but young and tender.'

'Good,' said the jolly-faced gentleman.

'Where do you live?' asked a very unjolly Guardian, and he put in a hem between every word.

I told him not far from the Duke of

York, and scarcely a stone's throw from the Free and Easy.

'Capital acquaintance with liquor shops', remarked the unjolly G.

'Known 'em all my life,' I said.

'Is your residence contagious to the Pope's Head?', asked the same party.

I replied 'There is no contagion in my dwelling that I know of, except that the other day there were five cases of fever near me, and four of 'em recovered, and I understand you gentlemen have been so generous as to pay the doctor for curing 'em after the rate of one and six per head!'

Unjolly G. appealed to the Guv'nor, 'whether he thought it proper that such unwarrantable observations should be made by an impertinent pauper.'

He actually called me 'imperent'.

The Guv'nor was rather deaf, and didn't hear unjolly G., which I think he contrived not to do on purpose.

'You should endeavour, pauper,' said the aforesaid unjolly G., 'always to distort your mind from such notions as you appear to me most unproperly to entertain.'

I replied by saying that I was sorry to observe a disposition on his part to distort every good thing I said.

'You are the most in-kor-ri-gi-ble party as ever was,' observed the unjolly G, 'and if I had my way you should have a month at the treadmill.'

'No, no,' said a number of the jollier sort – all in one breath. Christmas Day tomorrow, and how could you eat your roast beef and plum pudding in comfort if you thought this poor fellow was grinding the wind on a treadmill?'

'Hear, hear,' said the aforesaid jolly red-faced Guardian, and 'hear, hear' was echoed by several others, who I could see were accustomed to keep Christmas as Christmas always should be kept.

'We'll send our officer to investigate into your circumstances tonight,' said the Guv'nor, and 'You shall have a Christmas dinner if you deserve it, as I hope you do,' he continued.

'I am sure I do (I said) much more

than that old cove' – pointing to the unjolly Guardian.

'Mr Guv'nor, I rise to order,' said the individual in question, in a raging voice, and a stormy manner.

'You be blowed,' I said.

'Order, young man,' said a very little gentleman with a large head, in a mild tone, which I construed to mean *the behaviour of this young man is not strictly proper but I can't be hard upon him – tis Christmas day tomorrow*.

I bowed to the Guv'nor, and the Guv'nor bowed to me, and then I left, first casting a withering look on the unjolly G, who gnashed his teeth at me, and ejaculated 'The most imperent pauper as ever came before us!'

'Did I get relief? No, I didn't, for when the Relieving Officer came to my house he found a young woman (my wife) stuffing a jolly goose, and another young woman (my wife's sister) manufacturing a jolly pudding for the next day's dinner.

The head of the house was smoking his pipe, and drinking a glass of grog by the fire. That head was my honourable self.

What did I say to the R. O. Why I told him twas a lark, and I made him drink three glasses of stiff grog, thus flavouring and making piquant the joke, which he much enjoyed. The grog likewise prepared his mind for the due enjoyment of the festivities of the blessed season. As to unjolly Guardian, I sent him my compliments, and asked him to dine with me, but he 'treated the invitation with contumely (contempt) which it merited',

You ask me the moral of my story? Why this – that there are very good as well as very queer guardians of the poor in this free and happy country. How do you propose to amend the system? Put the right men in the right place.

PIXIE LED:
A CHRISTMAS
ADVENTURE ON
HALDON

UNKNOWN

1895

I'm what they call a Moor Farmer, and if
you know what that means, you won't
expect any grand speechifying in a yarn
from me; though my dear old missus,
who came in from over the hill, and had
a boarding school education in her
youth, has promised to look over this
when I've done and put it a bit ship-
shape. She says that I must tell it myself.

It was a matter of twenty years ago it happened. Twenty years ago, to be precise, come Christmas Eve! First of all I ought to say that I, and my father before me, have farmed the estate, on the border of Dartmoor, where I'm living now, for more than three quarters of a century. Me and my missus are well nigh seventy years old; so you see we were about fifty that Christmas. The bit of a farm we live on, and one five miles away, are both our own, as well as a good bit of wild uncultivated ground where we run ponies, so you see we're a little rich in this world's goods, some of us moor land farmers.

But we were not rich in one way.

We had no children. Two tiny mites had been given to us in the first four years of our married life, but they had both pined away, and died in infancy. It was the one crook in our lot, this lack of children's voices in our home.

All this has nothing to do with my story, you are thinking, but you will see.

I always make it a point to attend Christmas Market in Exeter, if I can. I don't go to Exeter I suppose more than half a dozen times in the year, but Christmas is always one of those times.

Well! Twenty years ago I'd had a bit of a cold the market-day, and my missus, she's a bit soft about me you know, and like to coddle me when I'll let her, had insisted that I must stay indoors for a day or two; so when it came to the morning of Christmas Eve, I couldn't realised that the next day would be Christmas Day, so says I:

'I think I'll go to Excter to-day, old woman!'

'Well! John,' says she, 'If you do, there are a few little things I want, and you can bring them.'

So I started on my old brown cob, with a thick muffler about my neck, that I shoved into my pocket as soon as I was out of sight.

'John!' my missus called after me. 'Be sure to be home early to burn the ashen faggot.'

With her last words in my mind I had left Exeter before five o'clock on my return journey, and was jogging comfortably along the Alphington Road with every pocket of my coat bulging with parcels, and one or two tied on to the saddle. As far as Alphington Church I had company, but there my friend branched off to the right, and I followed the straight road.

In Kennford village I stopped at the Anchor for a glass. It was very dark by then, and the landlord wished me joy of my long, rough ride.

But I laughed at his sympathy till he said:

'It's just the night for the pixies to

be abroad, you know.' I knew he was only laughing at the faith I shared with most of the old-world folks I'd been brought up amongst; which faith I hold still. I don't say the 'little people' are half so busy nowadays as they were when I was a boy. The railways, and telegraphs, and electric light, and the deuce knows what in the way of improvements, are enough to frighten them out of existence. But the pixies did some mighty queer things in my youth. Aye! and punished evil-doers, and rewarded the good, in a wonderful manner, too. Tell me the pixies never existed!

How was it we always had to mark

a cross on our heaps of newly-threshed corn else, but because they would have scattered it to the four winds, if we hadn't shown so that we knew who we had to thank for a plentiful harvest; see the men and women too, out of number, that I've known to be pixie-led in my youth. Old women going from work, who have had to wander, round and round a field, seeking the gate to go out, and passing it heaps of times, till the little people have chosen to cease their gaming, and let 'em go home. Last of all, haven't I been pixie-led myself? Wasn't I pixie-led that very Christmas Eve now twenty years ago? I'll tell you what happened after I left

Kennford, and you can judge for yourself.

It's a quiet, dreary ride over Haldon at night, and apt to be dangerous sometimes, but I knew no fear, mounted on my stout nag, and with my heavy, lead-weighted hunting whip in my hand. I left the twinkling windows of a farm-house in the valley on the right, about a quarter of a mile from the village, behind me and after that I was going up Haldon Hill.

Old Brownie went so slowly, jogging from side to side on the wide road; perhaps, too, that last glass had made me somewhat sleepy; at all events I don't remember any more till my horse tripped over a loose stone, and almost pitching me over his head, awakened me into full possession of my faculties. (That's my old woman's sentence, not mine.) I sat upright in a moment, pulled Brownie up, and then became aware of two things at once - that I was on the top of Haldon and that I had lost my hat.

Where I'd lost it I didn't know. You see I didn't remember anything after passing the entrance to Trehill grounds, and it might have fallen off almost directly after I began to doze.

It was always a long enough journey for Brownie without doubling over any of the ground, and I, too, was anxious to get home, so I made up my mind to leave the hat where it was, tied a knot in each corner of my red handkerchief, pulled it on my head and well down over my ears, and started on again. Or thought I was going to; and that's where the little people come in. The minute I caught up the rein I could feel their presence, and I wasn't so terribly surprised when Brownie just set his four feet stiff, and refused to stir.

For why, sir? Why because the little people wouldn't let him go on. Tell me! The pixies knew what they were about that night, I always think that one of them may have knocked my hat off. Anyway, Brownie refused to stir, and when I have him a gentle reminder with the whip, he just turned square round, and began to trot back down the very road he had come up. I didn't try to stop him, because I knew for certain now it was the pixies' doing, and when at last he broke into a walk, I took that as a sign that I must get off and look for my hat; it must be about here I had lost it.

So down I got and with Brownie's bridle over my arm began to poke about among the brambles, and fallen leaves with the butt end of my hunting whip. Presently I struck something hard and round, and stooped to pick up the hat. Before I could rise again my blood was suddenly frozen in my veins by a strange, unexpected noise. Yet it was only the wildness of the place, and the hour that made the sound at all alarming, for it was the cry of a little child.

It came, it seemed to me, from close to my feet, and after the first start of surprise was over, I drew aside the brambles and plunged into the ditch that ran along the side of the road, looking quite eagerly for the origin (my missus again) of the sound, that was by this time increasing.

At last I stumbled on a market basket, and, catching it up, was soon kneeling in the middle of the road, cutting the strings by which the cover was fastened down, with my clasp knife. It was as dark as pitch just there, for the great trees on both sides of the road met overhead, and low enough down to make even a short man like myself look out for his head in riding under them, so when I'd got the basket open I had to fumble about to find matches, before I could see what my treasure trove was like.

It had ceased crying now, and when I held a lighted match over the basket I found that it was a fair little baby about a year old. Her dear little head, all a mass of glistening curls, were pillowed on some warm, red stuff, and she was tucked in cosily enough, and dressed up very warmly, we found later on.

Suddenly, as I looked at her lying there so quiet, and looking up at me without a bit of fright in her blue eyes, some half forgotten baldames yarns of long ago concerning pixie challenges flashed into my head, and a strange, uncanny fear made me wonder whether she were a human child at all, or if I had not better leave her where I had picked her up.

I know I couldn't have done so, but, as if divining my thought she suddenly put up a tiny hand and grasped one of my big rough fingers as they rested on the edge of her basket, and stretched the other hand up to my face, with a little crow of delight.

She settled the matter then. I put the baby and hamper gently on quite old Brownie's back, jumped up carefully behind it, and so jogged home, Brownie going that way willing enough now. We rode into the farm-yard just as the kitchen clock struck twelve.

My missus was got very anxious, you may be sure, and perhaps the ferment she had been in about me made her receive the little burden I had brought home without a frown.

We advertised our find far and wide of course, but nobody sent to claim the child, though a few days after Christmas a letter came addressed to me in a strange writing, and when we opened it, there dropped out notes for £100 and a couple of lines.

'Take care of our darling, and bring her up as your own, and God will reward you.'

And we've done it, sir, and He has rewarded us, for she's been the sunshine of our home for twenty years. We've brought her up well, too, though I say it myself, and with her pianny, and her pretty French jabber, when she's a mind to it, she'd be no disgrace to her parents, whoever they are, though no one would claim her from us now, our pretty Noeline. That was the fine name my missus gave her, she said it was to do with her being found at Christmas time.

But I - in compliment to the little people who guided me to her that night - I have never called her anything but 'Pixie'.

The Christmas
in Devon Series

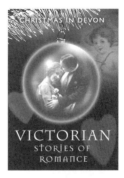

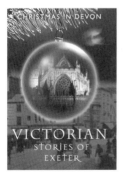

Also available from **The Mint Press**

Christmas in Devon (2001)
Victorian Ghost Stories
Victorian Stories of Romance
Victorian Stories of Exeter

Christmas in Devon   Todd Gray (2000)

The Devon Almanac   Todd Gray (2000)

The Concise Histories of Devon Series
Roman Devon   Malcolm Todd (2001)
The Vikings and Devon   Derek Gore (2001)
Elizabethan Devon   Todd Gray (2001)
Devon and the Civil War   Mark Stoyle (2001)

The Devon Engraved Series
Exeter Engraved: The Secular City (2000)
Exeter Engraved: The Cathedral, Churches, Chapels and Priories (2001)
Devon Country Houses and Gardens Engraved (2001)
Dartmoor Engraved (2001)

The Travellers' Tales Series
Exeter (2000)
East Devon (2000)
Cornwall (2000)